Dear Parents and Educators,

Welcome to Penguin Young Readers! As parents and educators, you know that each child develops at his or her own pace—in terms of speech, critical thinking, and, of course, reading. Penguin Young Readers recognizes this fact. As a result, each Penguin Young Readers book is assigned a traditional easy-to-read level (1–4) as well as a Guided Reading Level (A–P). Both of these systems will help you choose the right book for your child. Please refer to the back of each book for specific leveling information. Penguin Young Readers features esteemed authors and illustrators, stories about favorite characters, fascinating nonfiction, and more!

Miss Bindergarten and the Best Friends

LEVEL **2**

GUIDED READING LEVEL **E**

This book is perfect for a **Progressing Reader** who:
- can figure out unknown words by using picture and context clues;
- can recognize beginning, middle, and ending sounds;
- can make and confirm predictions about what will happen in the text; and
- can distinguish between fiction and nonfiction.

Here are some **activities** you can do during and after reading this book:
- Picture Clues: Sometimes pictures can tell you something about the story that is not told in words. Two of Emily and Vicky's classmates point out ways in which Emily and Vicky are not actually twins. Can you find other ways in which Emily and Vicky are not twins?
- Make Predictions: Vicky and Emily both wear blue coats, yellow boots, and red hats. What do you think they will wear tomorrow? Will they match? Work with the child to write a paragraph about Vicky and Emily's outfits.

Remember, sharing the love of reading with a child is the best gift you can give!

—Bonnie Bader, EdM
  Penguin Young Readers program

*Penguin Young Readers are leveled by independent reviewers applying the standards developed by Irene Fountas and Gay Su Pinnell in *Matching Books to Readers: Using Leveled Books in Guided Reading*, Heinemann, 1999.

For Morgan, almost one —JS

For Maria. We are *not* twins,
but we match!—AW

PENGUIN YOUNG READERS
Published by the Penguin Group
Penguin Group (USA) LLC, 375 Hudson Street, New York, New York 10014, USA

USA | Canada | UK | Ireland | Australia | New Zealand | India | South Africa | China

penguin.com
A Penguin Random House Company

Text copyright © 2014 by Joseph Slate. Illustrations copyright © 2014 by Ashley Wolff. All rights reserved. Published by Penguin Young Readers, an imprint of Penguin Group (USA) LLC, 345 Hudson Street, New York, New York 10014. Manufactured in China.

Library of Congress Cataloging-in-Publication Data is available.

ISBN 978-0-448-48132-6 (pbk)   10 9 8 7 6 5 4 3 2 1
ISBN 978-0-8037-3989-5 (hc)   10 9 8 7 6 5 4 3 2 1

PENGUIN YOUNG READERS

LEVEL **2**
PROGRESSING
READER

Miss Bindergarten
and the Best Friends

by Joseph Slate
illustrated by Ashley Wolff

Penguin Young Readers
An Imprint of Penguin Group (USA) LLC

Meet Miss Bindergarten.

Here is her class.

They call her Miss B.

One day at school,

Emily has a new blue coat.

Vicky does, too.

"I love blue," says Emily.

"I love blue, too," says Vicky.

"We match!"

9

The next day,

Vicky has yellow boots.

Emily does, too.

"I love yellow," says Vicky.

"I love yellow, too," says Emily.

"We match!"

The next day,

Emily has a red hat.

14

Vicky does, too.

"We match," says Vicky.

"We both have red hats,"

says Emily.

"You look like twins," says Miss B.

"Hello, twin," says Emily.

"Will you jump with me?"

"Yes," says Vicky.

"Hello, twin," says Vicky.

"Will you swing with me?"

"Yes," says Emily.

"We are twins!"

"You are not twins," says Gwen.

"Look, you have big ears."

"You are not twins," says Henry.

"Look, you have little ears."

"You are not twins," says Gwen.

"Look, you have a long nose."

"You are not twins," says Henry.

"Look, you have a short nose."

"We are not twins," says Vicky.

"We are best friends," says Emily.

"And we match!"